THE BIG STEW

Ben Shecter

A Charlotte Zolotow Book
An Imprint of HarperCollins*Publishers*

The Big Stew
Copyright © 1991 by Ben Shecter
Printed in the U.S.A. All rights reserved.
1 2 3 4 5 6 7 8 9 10
First Edition

Library of Congress Cataloging-in-Publication Data

Shecter, Ben.
  The big stew / by Ben Shecter.
      p.   cm.
  "A Charlotte Zolotow book."
  Summary: Two people get carried away making stew and turn into
witches.
  ISBN 0-06-025609-5. — ISBN 0-06-025610-9 (lib. bdg.)
  [1. Cookery—Fiction.   2. Witches—Fiction.]   I. Title.
PZ7.S5382Bi   1991   90-46271
[E]—dc20   CIP
                                                               AC

THE BIG STEW

Some days are stew days.

Today is a stew day.

I want stew.

We will make a stew.

A little of this;

a little of that.

Some more of this;

some more of that.

Not enough.

Not enough!

More.

MORE.

MORE!

Still not enough.

More that,

then this.

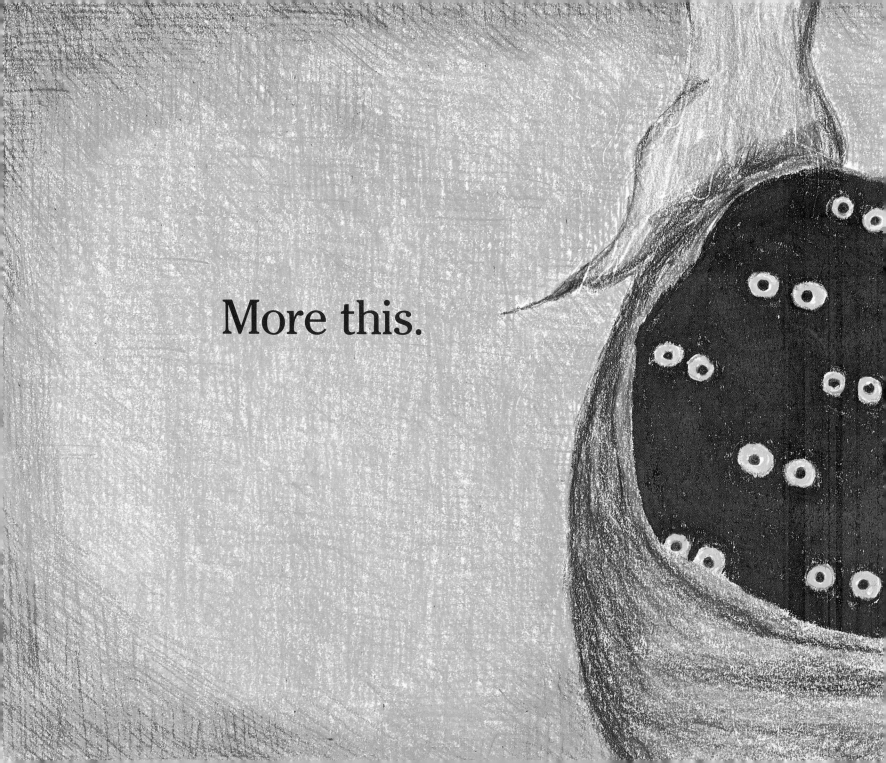

More this.

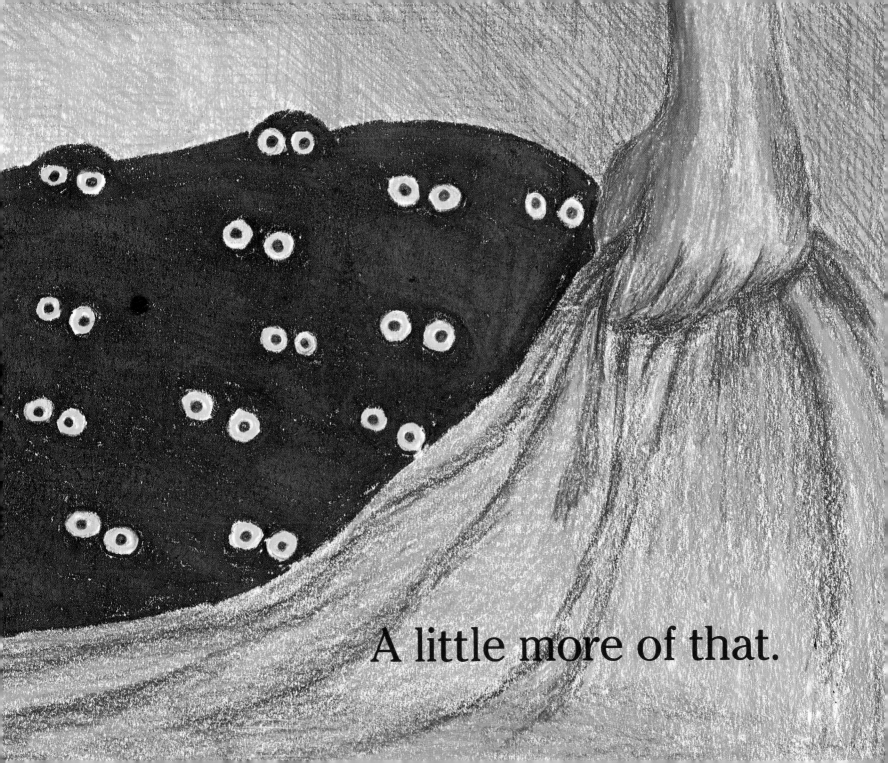

A little more of that.

That's not enough.

This will be enough.

Enough is enough!

TOO

Not too much   of this,

and not too much

of that.

Perfect!